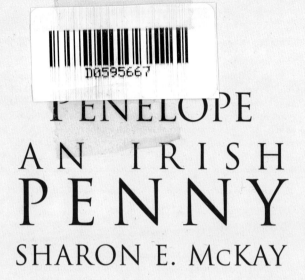

PENELOPE

AN IRISH

PENNY

SHARON E. McKAY

PENGUIN
CANADA

PENGUIN CANADA

Penguin Group (Canada), a division of Pearson Penguin Canada Inc.,
10 Alcorn Avenue, Toronto, Ontario M4V 3B2

Penguin Group (U.K.), 80 Strand, London WC2R 0RL, England
Penguin Group (U.S.), 375 Hudson Street, New York, New York 10014, U.S.A.
Penguin Group (Australia) Inc., 250 Camberwell Road, Camberwell, Victoria 3124, Australia
Penguin Group (Ireland), 25 St. Stephen's Green, Dublin 2, Ireland
Penguin Books India (P) Ltd, 11, Community Centre, Panchsheel Park, New Delhi – 110 017, India
Penguin Group (New Zealand), cnr Rosedale and Airborne Roads, Albany, Auckland 1310,
New Zealand
Penguin Books (South Africa) (Pty) Ltd, 24 Sturdee Avenue, Rosebank 2196, South Africa

Penguin Group, Registered Offices: 80 Strand, London WC2R 0RL, England

First published 2003

1 2 3 4 5 6 7 8 9 10   (WEB)

Copyright © Sharon E. McKay, 2003
Cover and interior illustrations © Ron Lightburn, 2003
Chapter opener illustrations © Ron Lightburn, 2003
Design: Matthews Communications Design Inc.
Map © Sharon Matthews

NATIONAL LIBRARY OF CANADA CATALOGUING IN PUBLICATION

McKay, Sharon E
Penelope : an Irish Penny / Sharon E. McKay.

(Our Canadian girl)
ISBN 0-14-301464-1

I. Title. II. Title: Irish Penny. III. Series.

PS8575.K2898P45   2003   jC813'.6   C2003-902887-9
PZ7

Visit the Penguin Group (Canada) website at **www.penguin.ca**

To Krystina,
Last but never least,
beautiful sister number three

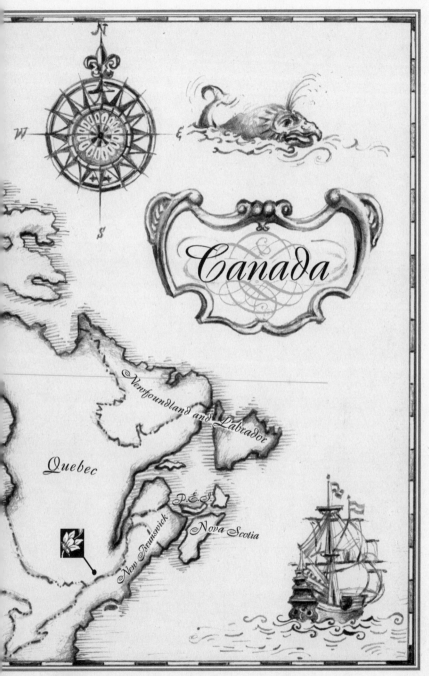

Canada

Newfoundland and Labrador

Quebec

P.É.I.

New Brunswick

Nova Scotia

Marks the location of the story

Penelope's Story Continues

WILL THE WAR EVER END? It's now the fall of 1918. French-speaking people in Quebec are mighty fed up with sending their sons into battle so far away, all to support the British, and there is talk of separating from Canada. Privately, many English-speaking Canadians right across the country are questioning this horrific war that has taken so many lives.

Penny is adjusting to her life in Montreal, but it's been a long, dreary summer. Penny's tutor has come almost every day, so that she'll be ready for school. It wouldn't have been so awful if she could have gone to see her sisters, Emily and Maggie, who are living with Papa's sister in Toronto.

Papa's letters say that he is working day and night to help rebuild Halifax. Penny is frantic with worry. What if he gets sick? After all, there is a dangerous influenza going around. Many nights she has cried herself to sleep.

A new school year is about to start, and Grandmother has enrolled Penny in Miss Potter's School for Girls. Going to a new school is always awful at first, and Penny hopes that she'll find a way to fit in. For some reason, the other girls make her feel that being Irish makes her somehow . . . different. And though Penny may not know anyone, everyone seems to know all about her.

"*Finished.*" *Aunt Colleen pushed a pin* into the pincushion and stood back to admire her handiwork. "As straight a hem as you're ever going to find. You look lovely, Penny."

"Thank you." Penny tugged at the waistband of her bloomers under her wool skirt, then twirled around to look at herself in the mirror. Her long red braid, bound by a dark blue ribbon, thumped on her back. There she stood, tall (she had grown a whole two inches), wearing a fitted white blouse, blue cardigan sweater with a school crest, and navy blue pleated skirt. She hardly knew herself. Maggie, almost two years old, might not recognize her. And then it occurred to her—Maggie too must have grown. Maybe they wouldn't recognize each other! That was silly, but it had been six months since she had last seen Papa, Emily, and Maggie. Did they miss her as much as she missed them? She couldn't help it. Tears brimmed in her eyes.

"Oh, sweetheart, the first day at a new school is always hard, but I promise, everything's going to be fine. Miss Potter's School for Girls is the finest in Montreal." Aunt Colleen looked into Penny's teary eyes, then hugged her. Penny managed to pull her lips into a tight, feeble smile.

"That's better. Well, it's a good try, anyway." Aunt Colleen smiled. "I shall write to your father this morning. I'll tell him how smart you looked on your first day at school. He is very proud of you, you know. And I'm sure you will fit right in. Mr. Davis says that you have made tremendous progress with your studies this summer."

Penny nodded. Most Montrealers summered up in the Laurentian Mountains, but Penny had spent a long, boring summer either pounding the piano with Miss Dockrill, her music teacher, or studying with Mr. Davis, the general tutor Grandmother had hired. The worst of it was not having any friends. Since saying good-bye to Maggie and Emily on the train early last spring, Penny had not actually talked to another child.

"Penny, your grandmother is waiting." Sally, wearing a starched cap and dressed in a crisp new black-and-white maid's uniform, stuck her head around Penny's bedroom door. She jumped back when she spotted Aunt Colleen. "Oh, excuse me, ma'am." In front of the family, Sally was always careful to say *Miss* Penny, instead.

"It's all right, Sally. Now, Penny, do you have your indoor shoes? Miss Potter is very strict about girls changing their shoes when entering the school." Penny nodded and patted her schoolbag. "And don't forget your tam. I shall be down for breakfast directly," said Aunt Colleen as she collected her thread and scissors.

Penny picked up her tam and schoolbag, then thumped down the stairs, with Sally hot on her heels.

"Let's have a look."

Sally took Penny's hat and bag and ran her eyes up and down as if she were a general inspecting the troops. At sixteen, she was only five years older than Penny, but there were times when Sally seemed much older.

"Ya look grand, so ya do. A regular toffee-face. Just like one of those posh girls."

"She does that." Duncan, balancing a large, covered silver tray on his shoulder, popped out through a door that led from the servants' staircase. "You're a picture!" And he winked as he sailed past the two girls towards the dining room.

"Ach, he's an ornament," whispered Sally. Both girls giggled. Duncan, at seventeen, was the footman, but he fancied himself the butler. He was thin and tall, with shoulders so broad that every few months Penny's grandmother had to send for Mrs. Hoffman, the dressmaker, to let out his uniform. He had flashing, dark brown eyes, a big smile, sandy-coloured hair, and he was awfully sure of himself. "Cocky as they come," is what Sally said of him.

Sally had known Duncan ever since she and her three brothers and father had arrived from Ireland. Duncan's family lived a few doors down from Sally's on Galt Avenue in Verdun. Verdun was one of the working-class neighbourhoods of Montreal. Duncan's family had come from Ireland, too. His father had been killed in an accident a long time ago, and both his older brothers were away in the war, one wounded and lying in a hospital in France.

"Where is my granddaughter?" Grandmother called out from the dining room.

"Go!" Sally grimaced, then gave Penny a gentle push through the doorway.

"Good morning, Grandma." Penny planted a kiss on her cheek.

Penny's grandmother was sitting at the end of the table. "Let me look at you," she said, then peered at Penny over her thin reading glasses. Why did everyone want to look at her? "You'll do," Grandmother pronounced with satisfaction.

Duncan removed the silver lid from the serving tray and Penny helped herself to eggs and sausages.

"Duncan, how is your mother?" asked Grandmother as she lifted a delicate teacup to her lips.

"Not very well, ma'am. Thank you for asking."

"Sally? Sally? Where is that girl?"

"Right here, ma'am." Sally bobbed up beside Grandmother's elbow and gave a small curtsy.

"Good heavens, girl, don't jump up at people like that. Tell Cook to make up a basket for Duncan's mother. Put in some of that blueberry jam from Maitland's."

"Yes, ma'am." Sally curtsied again while Duncan murmured a thank-you before one trailed the other out of the room.

Grandmother, as was the custom at breakfast, rattled off a list of things that had to be done that day, and then mentioned that she had sent a box of new winter coats and other clothes from Holt's to Emily and Maggie in Toronto. Toys, too. Penny nearly squealed with delight. Grandma peered over her glasses. Penny gulped. She didn't have to be reminded that young ladies and piglets should not make the same sounds.

Penny pushed her eggs around with her fork until she could make out the design on the plate. Would Emily and Maggie open the box by themselves? What she wouldn't give to see their faces. Penny looked towards the closed dining-room door. They were alone. Now would be a good time to talk about going home to Halifax, or maybe visiting Toronto. She just needed to find the right words.

"Grandma?"

"Yes, dear?" She looked up from her list. Grandmother's blue eyes had a way of looking right through her. "Penny, what is it?"

Penny's courage evaporated. "Pass the salt, please," she said instead.

"Good morning." Aunt Colleen, wearing a soft wool suit, snug at the waist, swept into the dining room. It was wonderful having such an elegant aunt. Of all the people in the world, not counting Papa and her sisters, Penny loved Aunt Colleen best.

"Penny," said Grandmother, "I meant to mention Gwendolyn Parker-Jones."

And as if on cue, Duncan appeared in the doorway and announced, "Miss Gwendolyn Parker-Jones." Standing directly behind him was a round, dark-haired girl with wire-rimmed glasses and a solemn expression.

"Good heavens, there you are, Gwendolyn. I was about to tell my granddaughter that you were coming to collect her. Well, come in, girl, don't just stand there."

"Good morning, Mrs. Underhill." The girl curtsied while looking at Penny out of the corner of her eye. Penny stared wide-eyed right back. Behind her glasses Gwendolyn had brown, sparkly eyes rimmed with thick lashes. She had a round face, ruby-red lips, dimples in both cheeks, and brown hair that was bound into two fat braids and tied with two navy blue ribbons.

"Penelope, dear, Gwendolyn has just got back from her holidays in the mountains. She will be in your form at school." Penny thought she heard herself say hello, but maybe not. "Won't you have a seat, Gwendolyn, while Penelope finishes her breakfast? Perhaps you would like a glass of juice? Sally? Sally? Where is that girl?"

"Here I am, ma'am." Once again Sally appeared at Grandma's elbow.

"Oh, for goodness sake. You'll give me a heart attack one day. Sally, would you please fetch Gwendolyn a glass of orange juice."

"No, thank you, Mrs. Underhill. We mustn't be late. Miss Potter takes a dim view of tardiness," said Gwendolyn.

Penny's heart sank. It was bad enough being new, but to be late, too—the thought was too much to bear.

"It is important to start the day with a good breakfast," Grandmother protested.

"Please, Grandma, I don't want to be late."

"But Arthur will drive you."

"Really, Grandma, it's a nice day, and if we leave now we'll be on time." Penny had no idea how long it would take to get to school, but the last thing she wanted was to arrive there in a chauffeur-driven automobile.

Penny ran around Grandmother's chair and landed a feathery kiss on her cheek. "Goodbye." She kissed Aunt Colleen, too.

"Be brave," whispered her aunt, reaching up to give her a quick hug before Penny could dash out the door.

"Penelope! Wait just a moment."

So much for a hasty escape. Penny stopped short as Grandmother rose and placed her napkin on her chair.

"Everyone, follow me." With Grandmother in the lead, Aunt Colleen, Gwendolyn, Sally, and Duncan trooped out into the front hall to give

Penny a proper sendoff. Sally plopped the tam on Penny's head and handed her the schoolbag.

Cheery goodbyes followed Penny and Gwendolyn down the drive to the road. Grandmother pulled a hanky from her sleeve and waved as if Penny were setting off on a great ship. Aunt Colleen, Sally, and Duncan were content with smiling and waving.

"You have a nice family," said Gwendolyn as they set off down leafy Pine Avenue. Penny looked over her shoulder. She could still see Grandmother's hanky waving in morning's early light.

"They are not my *real* family."

"They look real," laughed Gwendolyn.

"I mean that my *real* family is in Halifax. Well, my father is in Halifax. My sisters are staying in

Toronto until Papa builds us a new house. He's a builder."

"So, you have two families," said Gwendolyn in a matter-of-fact voice. "We've got lots of time, actually. Well, not *lots* of time, but it's all downhill. Come on. Step on a crack, break your mother's back." Gwendolyn took three big jumps across cracks in the sidewalk then pivoted in mid-air to face Penny. "Oh, I forgot, you don't have a mother. I don't have a father." Gwendolyn started to hop as if she were playing hopscotch on an imaginary board. "He got sick and died in France. He was too old for the war but he went anyway."

Gwendolyn made it sound as if having one parent were not a terrible thing. But it *was* a terrible thing, awful in fact. The only thing worse would be to lose *both* parents. The thought sent a shudder down Penny's spine.

"Do you miss your father?" Penny asked.

Gwendolyn shrugged. "He left at the start of the war, that was four years ago. I was only seven years old."

"My mother died one year and nine months ago. Sometimes I forget what she looks like." That was the truth of it, but it was the first time Penny had said it out loud. There had been no one to say things like that to for so very long.

Gwendolyn stopped jumping about. "There is a picture of my father at home on the mantel. I know it's him, but he doesn't look like the *him* I have in my head." Her shoulders slumped. "We're sort of the same, then," she said with a shy smile. "Call me Gwen. Gwendolyn sounds so old."

"I like to be called Penny. Penelope is my grandmother's name."

They walked on. It was a perfect fall day. The air smelled fresh and the leaves were just starting to turn colour. They talked about the test Miss Potter had given Penny over the holidays, and about Bloomfield School back in Halifax and how it was almost destroyed in the explosion.

Penny stopped walking and looked at her new friend. Gwen was staring wide-eyed at a house.

"What is it? What's wrong?"

"See him?" Gwen pointed to a man wearing a black uniform and a peaked cap. He was walking up the path towards a pretty, moss-covered house. The door was made of heavy oak. A large gold knocker gleamed in the morning sun.

"He's a mailman," shrugged Penny.

"No." Gwen shook her head. "He's delivering a telegram."

They watched while the man knocked at the door. A maid opened it, then fell back against the doorframe and shook her head. He handed her a yellow-and-blue envelope.

"That's how we were told that my father was dead in France. That's how everyone is told, by telegram. If a telegram arrives, it means that someone is dead, probably a soldier in the war."

The maid closed the door and the telegram man walked back down the path and out the gate, nodding to Penny and Gwen as he passed. Maybe they imagined it, maybe not, but as the girls passed the house they could almost swear that they heard an anguished scream echoing from its depths.

"Run!"

Gwen and Penny dodged a streetcar, two oncoming automobiles, several horse-drawn carriages, and steaming piles of horse droppings to race over the cobblestones of Guy Street. Their schoolbags, hanging by thin leather straps over their shoulders, banged against their hips.

Gwen raced past the white picket fence and thick hedge that stood in front of the school, a three-storey, red-brick Victorian residence with a sprawling white verandah. She ran up the steps and skidded to a stop so fast that Penny plowed

15

into the back of her. Nothing moved behind the pristine, white muslin curtains. That could mean only one thing. They were late.

"If Miss Potter catches us, we're in for a lecture for certain." Gwen, standing in front of the door, smoothed down the front of her fall coat with a flat palm. Penny did likewise. "Shoulders back, chest out. Ready?" Penny nodded. Gwen adjusted Penny's tam, then turned the door handle.

"Good morning, girls." Miss Potter, white-haired and small, yet commanding, stood in the school's entrance. Neither a smile nor a frown graced her face. "I trust your tardiness is a one-time event and will not be repeated."

"Yes, ma'am." Gwen gave a quick curtsy. "This is Penny Underhill."

"Penny Underhill Reid," said Penny shyly. Maybe a small smile flickered across Miss Potter's face then, but maybe not.

"Yes, Gwendolyn, Penelope and I met earlier this summer. Given that this is the first day, I will

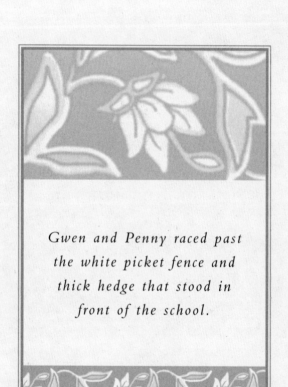

Gwen and Penny raced past the white picket fence and thick hedge that stood in front of the school.

dispense with a late slip. Off you go to morning assembly and prayers. Penelope, after assembly please come to my study. We will review your lesson plan for the year."

"Yes, ma'am." Like Gwen, Penny bobbed up and down.

Gwen charged into a cloakroom, with Penny not far behind. Dozens of dark coats and shoe bags hung from stubby pegs. Above each peg was a name and a square box that held hats and tams. On the floor beneath each coat were pigeon-holes for boots and bags and umbrellas, too.

Gwendolyn raced over to her peg and slipped off her outdoor shoes. "Hurry," she hissed.

Penny scanned the room looking for her name. Where was her peg?

"Just change your shoes. We'll find your peg later." Gwen dumped the contents of Penny's schoolbag on the bench. "Here." She tossed Penny a new pair of black, soft-soled shoes. "Hurry."

Penny's heart began to thump in her ears, and the more Gwen told her to hurry the more she fumbled about. She reached for her indoor shoes while Gwen gathered up Penny's outdoor shoes and shoved them in her own pigeonhole. According to Gwen, Miss Manning, the cloakroom mistress, was very particular about tidiness. They didn't need to get into trouble twice on the first day.

"Let's go."

Penny's feet were barely in her shoes before Gwen picked up her books and grabbed her by the hand. She stumbled out of the cloakroom and nearly fell over completely.

The two flew across the hall, where Gwen stopped outside a closed door, put her fingers to her lips and shushed. Morning prayers were held in the dining room.

When Gwen eased the door open, Penny could see that the room was full of bowed heads. Gwen tiptoed in first; Penny tried to do the same but almost tripped. A chair made a grinding sound on the wooden floor. Maybe all heads were bowed but it still felt as though all eyes were on her.

They slipped into the second-to-last row. Gwen handed Penny an Anglican Book of Common Prayer and both bowed their heads. Penny looked at her feet. She nearly passed out, fainted away entirely, died on the spot. She had her shoes on the wrong feet.

"Please sit down," said a tall, elegant lady with dark hair rolled in a bun and a long string of pearls around her neck.

"That's Miss Major. She's the second head," whispered Gwen.

Penny nodded, although she didn't know what a *first head* was, let alone a *second head*. She crossed her ankles and tucked her feet under her chair. From the row behind she heard the sounds *ire* and *shush*. Giggles floated up behind her like bubbles.

Gwen nudged her, motioned with her eyes to the row behind, and whispered, "That's Audrey Hicks. Don't pay any attention."

Penny bent her head down until her chin rested on her chest. *Ire* and *shush*? What did it mean? It came to her suddenly. *Irish*.

"Welcome back, girls." Miss Potter, now standing at the top of the room, clasped her hands together and beamed. "We hope that 1918 will be an outstanding year for our school. We have a few announcements, but first I'd like to welcome and introduce the new girls.

Dear God, Penny prayed, *please don't let her ask the new girls to walk to the front of the room. I will never ask for anything ever again. Please, God.*

"We'll start with the new girls in the lower school. As I call each girl's name, would she please rise and come and stand beside Miss Major."

"Dorothea Scott," said Miss Potter.

A small, curly-haired child bounced to the front of the room.

"Dorothea comes to us from British Columbia. It is Dorothea's seventh birthday today. I hope that you will all join me in welcoming her and wishing her a happy birthday."

Penny applied the toe of one shoe to the heel of the other. The shoe popped off and shot forward.

"What's wrong?" whispered Gwen.

Penny listed to the side and, without turning her head, whispered, "My shoes!"

Gwen leaned forward and spotted one shoe under the chair ahead and the other on the wrong foot. Even Gwen went pale.

"Constance Fitzgerald, would you please join me at the front of the room?"

A blond girl who looked to be about nine or ten years old stood up. How many new girls could there be? There were only a hundred girls in the whole school. Penny stretched out her toes. She couldn't reach the shoe under the chair. Gwen's prayer book landed with a resounding thud on the floor.

"Constance is from Toronto. Her father, Major William Fitzgerald, has just received the Military Cross while serving in France. I'm sure we all offer her our congratulations."

Gwen dropped to her knees and pretended to pick up her book. Penny popped off her other shoe.

Please, please don't say my name.

"Penelope Underhill Reid, where are you, Penelope?" Penny jolted forward. "There you are. Penelope comes to us from Halifax, Nova Scotia. As we are all aware, Halifax suffered a terrible explosion some months ago. I am sure we will all benefit from learning first-hand about what is now considered the greatest man-made explosion ever to occur on earth. Penelope, please come forward."

Gwen shoved one shoe, then the other, onto Penny's feet. Well shod, head held high, Penny walked to the front of the room and stood beside the two other new girls. Only Gwen noticed the wobble in Penny's walk.

"That's the heads' study. Their sitting and reception room is behind it. And that's the library across from it." Gwen pointed to each door as they filed out after morning prayers.

"Heads?" Penny envisioned heads on sticks behind the solid oak doors.

"I forgot. You used to go to a public school. Head of school is like a principal—that would be Miss Potter. Miss Potter is in charge of the day girls and she teaches Scripture. It's not horrible . . . well, not truly, truly horrible. We use Moulton's Modern Reader's Bible. It has all the 'begat' stuff in small type so you can just read the story. Miss Major is second head, like a vice-principal. She teaches elocution. *'O that I were where Helen lies, On fair Kirkconnel Lea.'*" Gwen put one hand over her brow and feigned some odd emotion or other.

Two of the littlest girls from the first form skipped past them. The little blond girl put Penny in mind of Emily.

"Young ladies do not run," rang out a singsong voice in the distance.

"How is your Latin? Miss Major is a bear about Latin. There's the stationery cupboard."

Gwen pointed to a cupboard under the stairs. "It opens at recess. Here's the study. Oh, wait." Gwen came to a stop. "I forgot my pencils in my schoolbag. I have to go back. I'll see you at recess." Gwen melted into the crowd before Penny could say another word.

Penny stood in the hall and peered into Miss Potter's study. It was an orderly room with two chairs pulled up in front of a small, coal-burning fireplace. A tidy desk was pushed up against a wall. There were several bookcases jammed with leather-bound books against a far wall.

"Hello, *Irish*."

Penny spun around. Who said that? She looked up and down the hall. A sea of white blouses and blue sweaters and skirts brushed past.

"Penelope."

Penny jumped, then looked up at Miss Potter.

"I didn't mean to startle you, dear. Come in and sit down." Miss Potter motioned to a chair by the fire and, with a file in her hand, sat in a chair beside Penny. "Now, let us discuss your academics."

Miss Potter pulled papers out of the file. Penny recognized the handwriting of her tutor, Mr. Davis.

"I must commend you on your diligence over the summer. Now, about your courses, you will study English Literature century by century, and you will be expected to have a comprehensive knowledge of Milton's *Paradise Lost* and Pope's *Essay on Man*. Of course, there will be poetry and French classics, along with French culture and French history. Then there is algebra, geography, drawing, science, grammar, composition, spelling, Scripture and ethics, British history, and so on. I am a little concerned about your Latin and Greek."

If Penny had discovered that her head were on backwards she would not have been in the least surprised. Mr. Shirley, her teacher in Halifax, had applauded when she'd said her six-times table without making a mistake. What would he think if he knew she was to study Latin and Greek?

"Penelope, are you listening?"

"Yes, Miss Potter."

"You look a little bewildered. Not to worry, all of this will become second nature to you soon enough. We are delighted to have you at our school. Remember, many of our girls have been here since first form. You will catch up, and your grandmother assures me that you will have tremendous support at home."

"Yes, Miss Potter."

"Come along. I shall take you to your first class."

Despite the fact that they sat beside each other at long wooden tables during class, Penny did not have a chance all day to talk to Gwen alone.

In calligraphy class a girl named Pippa, short for Philippa, mentioned that her grandmother and Penny's grandmother were both active members of the Imperial Order of the Daughters of the Empire. "That's the IODE," Pippa said with great authority. Penny nodded and wondered if Daughters of the Empire were royalty.

In French grammar class, Plum, which didn't seem to be short for anything, said that her mother and Penny's grandmother both sat on the Royal Victoria Hospital board. Penny nodded and tried to imagine her grandmother sitting on a hard board.

Over a hot lunch and quiet chatter, a girl named Felicity mentioned that Penny's mother and her mother had gone to school together. "That was before your mother ran away with . . ." There was a sudden hush. Felicity, whose hair was even redder than Penny's, turned pink, then peered down into her soup. All the girls at the table seemed suddenly entranced by the noodles that swirled around in their soup bowls. Even Gwen looked uncomfortable. Penny looked from one bent head to another. At last Penny, too, looked in her bowl. At least no one called her *Irish* again.

"I found your peg." Gwen pointed to Penny's name as the two girls entered the cloakroom. It was rather obvious, now that most of the girls had collected their coats and left for the day. Gwen and Penny changed their shoes, put on their fall coats, and headed out the door, too.

"What did you think?"

"Think about what?"

"About school, silly!" laughed Gwen.

"I think I will have lots of work to do." Penny paused. "Gwen, how did you know that I went to public school?"

It was Gwen's turn to pink up. "I just knew."

"I feel like everyone knows things about me, but I don't know about anyone else."

Gwen shrugged. "I guess everyone knows that your mother ran off with a poor Irishman . . ." She faltered. Penny swallowed hard. She couldn't think of a thing to say.

"I mean, your father's probably nice and everything, it's just that my mother said that your mother was the most beautiful woman in all of Montreal and that she could have married anyone, even royalty! My mother said that it was a terrible shame and . . ." Gwen's voice drifted. She didn't mean to hurt Penny's feelings.

Penny stood stone still. An image of Mama in the kitchen taking biscuits out of the oven rose up in her mind. Mama was smiling. Sometimes it was hard to picture Mama's face, and yet she could remember her smile without any trouble.

"Penny, I'm sorry. I didn't mean to make you cry."

Startled, Penny looked up. She hadn't realized that tears were rolling down her face.

"Does everyone know about my parents?" she whispered.

Gwen nodded. "I'm afraid so."

CHAPTER N°: 3

"Penny, dear, you have the day to yourself.
I trust you will use your time wisely."

"Yes, Grandma."

Grandmother stood in the front hall in her fall
wool coat, trimmed with mink, pulling on her
long, black calfskin gloves. "Colleen and I are
attending a meeting at the Royal Victoria
Hospital today. This overcrowding won't do.
Wounded soldiers deserve better than to be lying
on cots in hallways. I have told Cook to prepare
a light dinner for you. Ah, there you are, Colleen.
Arthur has brought the car around."

Aunt Colleen, dressed in a cream-coloured topcoat trimmed in white fur, descended the stairs while Grandmother looked around.

"Where is Sally? Sally!" Grandmother called up the stairs.

"Yes, ma'am." Sally popped up right behind her.

"Oh! Would you stop scaring me half to death? Now, I want the rugs in the back hall taken up, and what about the fireplaces? I think we should have them cleaned before Christmas."

Christmas. Penny's heart skipped. What would it be like to have Christmas without Papa and her sisters? It had seemed so far away before, but it wasn't, not really.

Grandmother and Sally put their heads together and talked about household matters. Sally was even fussier than Grandmother, and so the two were soon deep in conversation.

"Penny, are you feeling well? You look pale."

Penny nodded without really paying attention. Perhaps she could go home to Halifax for Christmas. No, that would leave out Emily and Maggie.

"Will you be all right by yourself?" asked Aunt Colleen.

Penny nodded again. Duncan and Sally, not to mention Cook, were all in the house. There might be even more servants lurking about the place for all Penny knew.

"I will be fine. Aunt Colleen, about Christmas."

"Yes, darling."

"I was wondering . . . I thought maybe if you asked Grandma about Papa coming for Christmas, and maybe Emily and Maggie . . ." Penny wavered.

Aunt Colleen reached out to Penny and touched her hair. "Have you mentioned this to your grandmother yet?"

"No, but . . ."

"Why don't you try? It's important that you talk to your grandmother. She loves you very much. Now, what about your history project, have you decided on a topic?"

"Not yet. Elizabeth Regina, maybe." The assignment was to write about a specific time or person in British or Canadian history and how that time or person changed the world. She was supposed to have her topic chosen by Monday morning, and today was Saturday.

"Queen Elizabeth, an excellent choice. Ruled with an iron fist, and if her subjects did not obey—off with their heads!" said Grandmother as she rejoined the conversation. Not for the first time, Penny thought that her grandmother would make a good queen.

"I have a letter here for your father. Do you want me to post yours along with mine?" asked Aunt Colleen.

Penny shook her head. "I haven't finished it yet," she said. Goodness, Aunt Colleen and Papa wrote to each other a lot.

"Come along, Colleen. Mrs. Meighen is chairing the meeting. We must not be late."

Aunt Colleen kissed Penny on the top of the head. "When you have finished your letter, take it downstairs to Duncan or Sally. It is their half-day off. They can drop it in a pillar box on their way to see their families in Verdun. We'll talk about Christmas later." Aunt Colleen whispered the last bit.

As the door closed behind them, Penny wafted into the living room, almost tripping over the telephone box on the floor. It was a perfectly appointed room. Two large, high-backed chairs sat beside the fireplace. There was a long, red velvet sofa and matching settee, plus several foot-stools, smack in the middle of the room. The tables and sideboards were all made of oak polished to a high shine, and the wallpaper was covered in small velvety flowers that bloomed winter and summer. It was a nice room, but not nearly as cozy and pretty as the sitting room that she and Mama had decorated in Halifax.

It didn't take long for Penny to finish her letter to Papa. She tucked it into an envelope, then went downstairs in search of Sally.

"What brings the young mistress of the house down to visit us poor serfs?" Duncan, grinning as usual, was sitting on a small stool by the back door polishing his boots. Sally, wearing a long, light-brown apron, was hunched over the deep kitchen sink. Her sleeves were rolled up past her elbows, and the steam from the hot water had turned her nut-brown hair frizzy.

"I've finished my letter."

"Pop it in my bag. I'll post it on my way," said Sally, as she twisted every droplet of water out of a cloth then hung it on a line in front of the fire.

Penny dithered, then plopped down on a bench beside a wooden table that nearly ran the length of the kitchen. She liked the kitchen. It was old fashioned and rather dark, but there were lots of shiny copper pots about the place. And the fire in the grate made it lovely and warm. She yawned. There was positively nothing to do. Well, nothing interesting, anyway.

"I was wondering if I could come with you to Verdun?" In truth, Penny hadn't been wondering at all. The idea had just popped into her head. But once she'd said it, she knew that it was exactly what she wanted to do. "I wouldn't be any trouble, and I have done all my homework. Oh, please?"

"And what would Lady Muck think if she knew we had taken her precious granddaughter down to mix with the Irish working class?" Sally pretended to be shocked. Duncan just threw his head back and laughed.

Was she precious? Aunt Colleen said that Grandmother loved her. But the truth was, Penny didn't *feel* very loved, at least not by Grandmother.

"Please?" she tried again.

"I think not," said Sally.

"What's the harm?" asked Duncan as he pulled on his boots.

"Ach, Duncan, have ya lost what little mind ya had in the first place?"

"And who might this girl's father be? Is he not Irish just like us? And if she's half Irish, then I'll tell you straight, it's the better half of her." Duncan's eyes were blazing. Being *in service* and catering to mucky-mucks rubbed him the wrong way. But with his brothers off fighting the war, it was up to him to care for their widowed mother as best he could. Except for a few coins held back for bus fare and a pint or two, every cent he made went to her.

"Now then, my girl." Duncan bent down and stared into Penny's green eyes. "If we took ya with us, would ya be able to keep it to yourself?"

Penny nodded her head vehemently.

Sally turned around so fast that the soap from her hands splattered on the stone floor. "Think what you're doing, man. Are ya not teaching the girl to lie?"

"But Sally, it's not lying if you are not asked a question, is it? If Grandma doesn't say, 'Did you go to Verdun with Sally and Duncan?' then it's not really, really lying if I don't tell her, is it?" Truth be told, Penny wasn't thinking that far ahead. It was just so boring being alone in the house.

"Don't split hairs, my girl," said Sally as she rubbed a cloth up and down her arms.

"Now what would you want to leave her alone for in this great blooming box of a house? And who's left to take care of her? Sure we're doing the right thing."

"Cook is here," said Sally, but her voice was wavering.

"That old trout is sleeping. Sure she hasn't been awake for longer than a meal in years."

"What about the influenza? There's many a house in Verdun that's come down with it. And wasn't your own Mum nearly taken off with it just last spring?" Sally was clearly upset.

"There's no more chance of Miss Penny here getting the influenza down in Verdun than there is at that fancy girls' school they packed her off to. Go get your coat, girl. You can come along. But mind, you're not to say a word to your grandmother. Promise?"

Penny could actually hear Sally suck in her breath.

"I promise."

Penny raced out of the kitchen, taking the stairs two at a time, before Sally could say another word.

CHAPTER N⁰ 4

Wicker baskets dangled off Sally's and Duncan's arms as the three hustled down the steep hill towards St. Catherine Street. Montreal's main street was jammed with noisy automobiles, carts and horses, and streetcars, too. The road was covered with horse dung and the sidewalks were packed with shoppers. It was exciting. There was so much to look at that Penny could hardly keep her head on her shoulders. If she'd been littler she'd have jumped up and down.

Penny looked up at Sally's sour face. Her mouth was turned down and puckered up, both at the same time. She became even more annoyed when Duncan told her that she looked like she was sucking lemons.

"That's ours," said Duncan as he pointed to an oncoming streetcar. Sparks flew off the overhead lines and its wheels shrieked as it came to a grinding halt. The three hopped on and hardly had time to sit before they had to change street-cars at Atwater and head down the hill towards the St-Antoine Market.

A dozen or so horses, carts, and wagons stood around the long, sandstone building. The outdoor fruit and vegetable market had closed up for the winter. Duncan pulled open the heavy wooden door. The place was bustling. Before them was a long, enormous hall. English and French voices called out, making a whole new language. Vendors cried out and chickens clucked up a storm in their wicker cages. Whole cows hung from great, black hooks—pigs and goats, too. Men wearing leather smocks, with mighty muscles bulging under their shirts, grunted and grimaced as they hauled giant cubes of ice pinched between giant ice hooks. Soupy-eyed fish lay on beds of crushed ice. War restrictions on food, especially meat, meant more people were eating fish. Of course, people in Halifax ate loads of fish, but it was different in Montreal.

It didn't take long for Sally and Duncan to fill their baskets with tea, biscuits, potatoes, brown flour, a pound of oatmeal, a few fall apples, and a strip of bacon each. And just as they were about to leave the market, Duncan stopped and bought a single red rose. Sally—her mouth now in a near-permanent pout—said that his mother would not be thanking him for wasting his money, especially since roses were very dear out of season. Duncan just flashed her a big, toothy grin.

They clambered back onto another streetcar. Sally and Penny sat on a bench with the baskets on their laps. Duncan stood, rocking back and forth on his heels while holding on to a leather strap that dangled overhead. The streetcar crossed

a newly constructed swing bridge over the aque-
duct that led into Verdun.

"Can ya see the Queen Victoria Bridge
through the houses?" said Duncan. "It's a beauty.
As tough and strong as the old lady it was named
after. Wouldn't I like to build such a thing."

Penny looked over her shoulder. The bridge's
black struts looked bold and fierce against the blue
afternoon sky. Of course, she had crossed it by train
when she'd first arrived. Montreal was an island,
after all. But she could never have imagined how
powerful it looked. It stretched clear across the
St. Lawrence River all the way to the South Shore.

Sally, looking straight ahead, sat with her
mouth clamped firmly shut. She had barely
spoken a word since they had left the house, but
her thoughts were plain enough. There would be
some to-do if Mrs. Underhill found out that
Penny had visited Verdun without permission.

The streetcar's wheels squealed and the three
got ready to hop off as it stopped at the corner of
Galt and Wellington Avenue.

The houses up and down Galt were nearly identical. They were tiny and mean looking and mostly made of brick. The front doors opened directly onto the small sidewalks. There wasn't a blade of grass in sight. They were called "two up and two down" on account of the two rooms downstairs, a parlour and a kitchen, and the two bedrooms upstairs. Sometimes there was a box room for storing things, too.

Children, boys mostly, ran up and down the cobbled stone road chasing each other and tossing balls back and forth. A sorry old livery horse clomped by. The driver sat in a rickety old flat-bed cart. The reins hung from his hands and his chin bounced off his chest.

"Ach, would ya look at that," laughed Duncan, and then he called out, "Mr. O'Brien, have ya finished your deliveries then?"

The driver jolted up, looked about him, grinned sheepishly, and then hollered, "Just twenty winks is what I'm after there, Duncan-boy. 'Twas a mite easier when I had your help, I'll be telling ya." Horse and driver plodded on.

Sally waved to two women standing in door-ways. Both smiled and waved back.

"Sally's Da lives over there, and my ol' Mum lives five doors down." Duncan pointed out their homes with pride.

"Will ya take her to see your Ma, then, Duncan?" Again that worried, lemon-sucking look crossed Sally's face.

"My ol' Mum would be delighted to make the acquaintance of Miss Penelope Underhill of Montreal." Duncan tipped his cap and bowed to Penny.

Penny giggled, curtsied, then said that her name was Penny Reid and that she was from Halifax, thank you very much.

"Well, I dare say she would like to meet both Penelope Underhill *and* Penny Reid."

"I'll stop by and pick you two up later," Sally said. "Don't you go forgetting, we must get back before Mrs. Underhill does."

"Do ya think that we are in the company of a

worrywart, Penny?" Duncan laughed.

Sally knitted up her forehead and grumbled, but that made Duncan laugh all the more and he said that if she kept up with her carry-on the lines on her forehead would stick and then he would be the only one who would have her. Sally still scowled, but this time there was just a hint of a smile on her lips, too.

Duncan flung open the door and hollered down a dim hall. "I've brought you a gift, Mother." A thin, merry voice called back and bade him come in.

Duncan's hand propelled Penny down a narrow hall, and soon she stood peering into a cheery, tiny room. Two comfy chairs were tucked up by a poor fire. The walls were painted a soft yellow and there were lots of knick-knacks about the place. The place smelled of lemon wax and linseed oil.

"Ach, Mum, it's freezing in here. Sure haven't I told ya that you've got to keep warm if you're to get well? And haven't I paid the coal man to the end of the month? You've got plenty to use up." Duncan charged over to the grate and shoved bits of coal onto the fire.

"Why would I be wasting coal when there's only me about the place and it's not even October?" The smiling little woman, with a crocheted shawl about her shoulders, put down her knitting and cocked her head to one side. She was as thin as paper, with skin so pale it was almost see-through. Her hair was thick, not white like Grandmother's but sparkling silver.

"Miss Penelope Reid, meet my dear ol' Mum, Mrs. O'Malley." It became apparent that Penny, not the basket of food or the rose, was his Mum's present.

"How do you do? You can call me Penny if you like."

Mrs. O'Malley tilted her head. Her entire face crinkled up into a big smile. When she reached out her hand, Penny took it and curtsied.

"Ach, she's a lovely wee thing."

"She's Mrs. Underhill's granddaughter," said Duncan.

Mrs. O'Malley looked genuinely shocked. "Duncan, are ya telling me that the likes of Mrs. Underhill lets her granddaughter visit these parts?"

"My father is Irish." Penny rushed in before Duncan could say another word.

"Is he now? Take your coat off and sit yourself down." Mrs. O'Malley still had a worried look on her face.

"Seeing as you have company, Ma, I'll make the tea then do the chores. Now don't you go filling her head with stories about the old country." Duncan added more coal to the fire then swaggered off down the hall whistling a tune.

"He's a good boy, so he is," said Mrs. O'Malley as she gazed at Penny. Her eyes were milky but kind.

"Duncan says that you are from Ireland?" Penny felt suddenly shy.

"Indeed I am."

"Why did you come to Canada?"

"Sure Ireland was a grand place but a hard one, too. I came to Canada to give my children a better life. And look where they are, two off to the war in France and another one working in service. I'll be happy when we are all back together again."

"Can you, would you, tell me about Ireland?"

"Tell you about Ireland? Oh, my dear, nothing would give me greater pleasure." Mrs. O'Malley gazed into the fire that now glowed brightly and made the tiny room cozy and warm. But she was not seeing the fire. She had a look that Papa sometimes got when he talked about Ireland, a far-off look of longing.

"I mind my father sitting by the turf fire puffing on his clay pipe and telling stories of mighty giants, of fairies and leprechauns and all things in between heaven and earth. You see, my dear, Ireland was an empire, not of marching soldiers and mighty armies, but of the imagination."

Penny stared into the fire, and for a moment she could see giants, fairies, and leprechauns leaping among the coals.

Penny, too, stared into the fire, and for a moment she could see giants, fairies, and leprechauns leaping among the coals.

"And how are my two girls getting along?" Penny jumped. "Tea, soda bread, and jam at the ready." Duncan stood on the doorsill holding the tea tray, complete with the rose in a jam jar. His sleeves were rolled up and an apron was wound around his waist. "Are you filling this wee one's head with nonsense, Ma?" he asked, his voice crackling with laughter. He put the tray on a small serving table by Mrs. O'Malley's elbow. "Mind that pot, Ma. It's hot."

This is what my home in Halifax used to be like, thought Penny. She snuggled back into the snug chair. Everything here felt good, felt *right*.

"I bought ya a wee flower here, Mother," said Duncan.

"Ach, Duncan, do ya not have a better place to spend your money?" Mrs. O'Malley scolded him but she was smiling all the same.

"A lovely red rose for my darlin' ol' Mum. Take a sniff." Duncan brought the flower over to his mother and held it under her nose.

"Oh, it's lovely, Duncan. Thank you."

"I'll just put it here in the window so the neighbours can think you're being courted by some old fella." Duncan winked at Penny then placed the rose on a three-legged table right smack in the middle of the small bay window that faced the street.

"Do you like soda bread?" Mrs. O'Malley asked Penny as she poured out the tea.

"My mother used to make it for my Papa," said Penny softly.

"Did she now?"

Penny nodded. She hadn't tasted soda bread since Mama had died. It seemed like a lifetime ago.

"Carry on, girls. I'll tend to this house. I'm just a poor brute of a man fit only for work," said Duncan as he headed back towards the kitchen. Mrs. O'Malley beamed after her son.

She turned to Penny again. "Would you be taking milk and sugar in your tea, then?" Mrs. O'Malley asked formally.

"Yes, please." Penny nodded.

"Now, what can I tell you about the old country, for sure there's a lot to tell." Mrs. O'Malley passed over Penny's cup.

Penny lowered her head. She wanted to ask why it was that people called the Irish *dirty,* and why there were signs saying "Hiring. No Irish Need Apply" in some shop windows. And it wasn't just in Montreal, either, it was in Halifax, too, and in plenty of other places no doubt. Why?

"Might ya be knowing that without Ireland the great books of the world would have been lost forever?" Penny's mouth gaped open. "Ah yes, when the world ran to wrack and ruin, 'twas the great scribes of Ireland that collected, copied, and preserved the world's books. For no one thought at the time to conquer the wee green island and it was left to itself. There the great knowledge was protected. And when the world came back to itself a hundred or more years later, and civilization once again came round, it was Ireland that gave back the books, gave back the knowledge. Without these books, the world that we live in today would be sorely different.

"How do you know?" Penny leaned forward, her elbows on her knees.

"Know what, my girl?"

"That it's true—about the Irish, about them saving the books?"

"Every generation passes the stories down to the next. We are storytellers all."

"Am I a storyteller?"

"If ye be Irish, it's in your blood. Ya cannot help telling a story." Mrs. O'Malley's eyes twinkled. "It drives the Canadians a little mad, I think, when they ask an Irish person the time of day or the state of the weather and out comes a tale."

"Then why . . . ?" How could she say it? "Why do they call the Irish *dirty*?"

The word hung in the air. It was as if a dark cloud had passed over the old woman, for her face fell. For a moment neither spoke. Penny grew hot with shame. She shouldn't have asked. She had spoiled everything.

"Ach, dear, where did ya hear a thing like that? Sure aren't some folks hard the whole world over? But I'll tell you if I can. There is a saying in dear Ireland that goes, 'May your hand be stretched out in friendship and never in want.' There came a time when the hand of Ireland was stretched out in want and there was no friendship to be had." Mrs. O'Malley took a deep breath. "Between the years of 1845 and 1851, a mere seventy years ago or thereabouts, the Great Hunger came to dear Ireland. My own father was a boy. He lost his brothers and sisters to starvation. Can you think what it must have been like, to watch your children, your brothers and sisters too, die of hunger? Think of a father holding his son or daughter as the child lay dying."

Penny took in a breath. She remembered Papa's eyes, wild with fear, when he'd found his three girls after the Halifax explosion. What would have happened if he had found three small bodies instead?

"Why were the Irish people hungry? Could they not grow more food?" Penny's voice was just a whisper.

"The potato is what we Irish grew. When it turned black and foul with rot, the poor peasants had no food to eat nor money to pay the landlord's rent. Old and young alike were turned out of their cottages to die along the roadside. The lucky ones found passage to Canada, to America, and to Australia, but many a poor soul died of disease on those ships, for the conditions were desperate. Think of the tears as they lay sick and dying in the filthy holds. Small wonder the sea is salty. And when they arrived didn't they unknowingly spread the disease to the people who lived in Canada. Poor wee Halifax, Montreal, too. Hundreds were lost, and so these Irish souls were called *dirty* when all they were was ailing."

Penny's heart sank when she heard the word

Halifax. It wasn't fair and it wasn't right that people still called the Irish *dirty*, but now she understood.

"Penny, we're that late. Oh, good evening, Mrs. O'Malley." Sally, flushed and puffing, stood in the doorway. "I got caught up with the chores. Where is Duncan?"

Penny looked past the rose and out the window. It was almost dark outside. She hadn't noticed the passing of time, not a bit!

"Duncan, Duncan!" Sally hollered down the dim hall towards the kitchen. "Quick, Penny, put on your coat. I'm sorry to be rude, Mrs. O'Malley, but we must get Penny back where she belongs." Sally charged down the hall in search of Duncan.

"May I visit you again?" Penny stood up and put on her coat.

"My dear, there is nothing I would like more."

"Would you tell me more about the books, the ones the Irish *scribbers* saved?"

"The Irish *scribes*. Yes indeed."

"Penny darlin', come along." Sally was back. Duncan brushed past her carrying a tray.

"Well, Mum, it was good that wee Penny kept you company, for didn't I get the kitchen floor washed, cleaned the drain and the gutters as well, filled the coal bin, and made your dinner." Duncan shifted one tray then parked another in front of his mother.

"Duncan, hurry." Sally hopped from foot to foot like a child needing to pee.

"Yes, yes." Duncan kissed the top of his mother's head. "I'll be back on Saturday afternoon."

Mrs. O'Malley lifted her frail hand and drew it across her son's face. "It was a lovely gift you brought me today. And Penny dear." Mrs. O'Malley turned towards her, "May the blessings of each day be the blessings you need most. Now off with you."

Sally needed no more encouragement than that, for she grabbed Penny's hand and flew out the door and down the road.

"Goodbye, goodbye," Penny called over her shoulder.

Duncan came scrambling up behind just as the streetcar arrived. The three jumped onto it and plunked themselves down in the wicker seats.

"Duncan, what did your mother mean when she said that blessing?" Penny asked.

"Oh sure it's an old Irish saying passed down from one generation to the next. She might well have said, 'May you be in Heaven half an hour before the Devil knows you're dead.'" Duncan winked.

"Can you not keep a civil tongue in your head, Duncan O'Malley? There's no need to teach the girl such things." Sally was back to fuming, which set Duncan to laughing all over again.

"You did my mother good today," said Duncan to Penny after he had calmed down a bit. "It's hard on her, being blind and all."

CHAPTER №6

"*Grandma, about Christmas. I was* wondering if Papa, Emily, and Maggie could come to Montreal." Sitting at the breakfast table, Penny held her breath.

"Christmas?" Grandmother ran her eyes down her "things to do" list. "That reminds me, Penny, I have told the charity committee that assembles the Christmas baskets for the poor that you would help. It's expected of us. 'From those to whom much has been given, much is required,' or so the Bible tells us. You may make the baskets up but under no circumstances are you to volunteer to distribute them. There is too much of this flu about and I don't want you down in places like Verdun." Grandmother paused and looked up.

"I'm sorry my dear, what did you ask?"

Penny paused and took a deep breath. "About Christmas and Papa and Maggie and . . ."

"Oh yes, we'll pack lovely gifts for them, too. You will be very busy this season. Then there are the Christmas parties. Of course, it's not what it was before the war, one simply must scale down, but you will find yourself occupied. You may want to have a small Christmas gathering of your own with the girls from school, an afternoon tea perhaps. I'm sure Cook will do you justice."

Penny didn't trust herself to speak. Her eyes were wide and round and her lips quivered. She peered down at her plate. What did she care about parties? Christmas without Papa or her sisters . . . how? Penny dabbed—she was careful not to wipe—her lips with her napkin. It took all she had to hold back her tears. She counted to ten, and when she was sure the lump in her throat had subsided she said, "Grandma, may I go to the Westmount Public Library on my way home from school today? I want to work on my history paper." Penny didn't look up; she didn't dare.

"Do you know where the library is?" Grandmother jotted down notes on the pad of paper by her plate.

"It's on Sherbrooke Street. I can walk there." From the inside of her head it sounded as though her voice wobbled. But Grandmother didn't seem to notice.

"Very well." Grandmother didn't look up. Instead she opened her newspaper and read for a moment while Penny tried to finish her breakfast. "Waste not, want not," that's what Sally always said, although Penny didn't know what it meant. Maybe it was another Irish saying.

"Between the wounded soldiers back from the war and this Spanish influenza, the hospitals are so overcrowded in Vancouver that they are using the University of British Columbia as an infirmary. Five hundred and twenty-two new cases have been reported. Duncan? Duncan, there you are. Tell Arthur I want the car brought around and ask Sally to fetch my bag from the dresser." Grandmother looked back down at the paper. "It's in Ottawa, too, and Montreal, I dare say. Of course, it all started in Quebec's Victoriaville College. Four hundred came down with it there. What can be done? And look at the price of medicine. Camphor once sold for 40 cents a pound and now it's selling for $6.50. They are running out of nurses and doctors everywhere. We must have an emergency hospital meeting today."

Duncan appeared with Grandmother's coat and gloves, Sally had run upstairs and fetched Grandmother's purse, and now all conspired to help her on her way.

"Arthur is pulling the car up now, ma'am," said Duncan.

"Sally? Sally? Oh, there you are. Stop disappearing and reappearing. I will be late tonight.

Have Cook prepare a cold dinner. I shall telephone if I change my mind. You *will* answer the
telephone, won't you, Sally?" Grandmother gave
Sally a stern look. Sally positively hated the telephone. The ringing unnerved her, and listening
to a voice without a body attached seemed
unnatural.

"Yes, ma'am," said Sally.

"Thank you, Duncan." Grandmother slipped
on her coat. "Penny? Penny!"

"Yes, Grandma." Penny stood in her school
coat. Gwen would be by to pick her up at any
moment. She had to speak to Miss Major before
morning prayers. There was no telling where
Miss Major might be by the afternoon. Like
everyone else, Miss Major not only worked in
the school but did her share of volunteer work as
well.

"You are sure you know how to get to the
library?" her grandmother asked.

"Yes, Grandma." Lies, all lies.

"I have to see Miss McBride about my music test. Save me a seat in prayers." Gwen dug out several loose music sheets and charged out of the cloakroom.

Penny hung up her coat, then thumped down on the bench to slip on her indoor shoes. She couldn't stop thinking about Christmas, and the more she thought about it, the worse she felt. It was all because Grandma didn't like Papa. Penny wanted to crawl away someplace and just cry. No, not cry, hit something. It was just so mean of Grandma. It was so unfair. But there was no time to feel sorry for herself. She had only a few minutes before prayers. Penny opened her book bag and pulled out some blotting paper, extra pen nibs, and exercise books.

"If it isn't the Irish potato-digger's daughter." Audrey Hicks stood in the doorway of the cloakroom. Her mouth was curved up in a grin.

Penny leaped up onto her feet and clenched her fists by her sides. Her temper flared like a match as she glared into Audrey's stone-hard eyes.

"Don't say that about my father. Don't *ever* say anything mean about my father."

"Penny?" Gwen bobbed up behind Audrey. Penny and Audrey's eyes were locked. Neither girl moved, but Audrey blinked first. She muttered something that sounded nasty that neither Penny nor Gwen could make out, then pivoted on her heels and stomped out of the cloakroom.

"I forgot my music textbook." Gwen's eyes were round with astonishment. "Was that really you?" She stifled a giggle.

"I guess so." Penny looked at her friend with equal amazement. Never, in her whole life, had she thought that she could stand up to someone like Audrey. Thing was, the words just popped out of her.

"You were amazing!"

Penny slumped down on the bench. She wouldn't let anyone say unkind things about her father. He was the nicest father in the whole world. Why couldn't she just go home?

Penny's heart pounded. It thumped so loudly in her ears that she could hardly hear, let alone think. She had lied to Grandma and Gwen. And she had *sort of* lied to Aunt Colleen and Sally and Duncan, too—that is, if not telling the truth was the same as lying. And now she had lied to Miss Major as well. She had surprised her by telling her the truth about the unusual subject she'd chosen for her project, but not about how she planned to study it.

"The research will be difficult, but a visit to Westmount Library is a good start," Miss Major had told her. "Also, there is a professor at McGill University who might be of help to you." Miss Major wrote out the professor's name. "This is most unusual," she'd said, her eyes twinkling, "but then we are a most unusual school."

It would all work out, Penny felt sure of that. Everyone would understand in the end, and maybe, just maybe, no one would ever find out about her fibs. Anyway, they really were *fibs,* not *lies.* Lies were meant to harm people, fibs were to protect people—or were they? It was so confusing. If only she could stop her heart from pounding. The streetcar passed the St-Antoine Market, crossed the swing bridge, and rumbled into Verdun.

"Excuse me." Penny stopped the conductor. "Could you tell me where Galt Avenue is?"

"Next stop, miss."

A minute later Penny stood on the corner of Galt and Wellington. Which house was it? They seemed to be identical. She turned and twisted around like a small tree in the wind. Women, wearing kerchiefs and aprons, stood on their doorsteps gaping at the girl dressed in a posh school uniform. A group of scruffy boys whistled in her direction. Penny tucked her chin into her coat, clutched her schoolbag, and plodded on down the street. Then she spotted it. The red rose Duncan had bought for his Mum was still in the window. What a relief.

She took a deep breath and knocked at the door. There was no answer. What if she had come all this way and no one was home? She knocked again then tentatively, slowly, turned the door-knob.

"Hello?" Penny called down the hallway. "Hello?"

"Come in." Mrs. O'Malley's singsong voice reverberated down the hall.

Penny was almost breathless when she burst into the tiny sitting room. The darkness of the room surprised her, but that was silly. Of course it would be dark. Mrs. O'Malley was blind.

"I came for a visit."

"Is that you, Penny?" Mrs. O'Malley reached out a thin, vein-lined hand.

Penny grasped it warmly. "I came to hear about the books, the ones the Irish saved."

"Did you now. And where is Duncan?"

"I came on my own." Penny was triumphant.

"You came by yourself?" Mrs. O'Malley gripped the arm of her chair and leaned forward.

"Yes. I often took the streetcar on my own in Halifax. I took care of my sisters, too, after my mother died."

"Duncan told me your story, dear girl." Mrs. O'Malley's voice was full of sadness. "No matter how rich or poor, every life carries its burdens. Might you light the lamp and make us a pot of tea?"

"I will." Penny, glad of the chores, put her coat and schoolbag on a chair and lit the lamp on the wall.

"Stick your head out the door and call for Jamie. He's a young boy who often helps me. Ask him to come in."

Penny dashed to the door and spotted a boy of perhaps nine years of age playing with a hoop and a ball on the road.

"Is your name Jamie?" Penny called out.

"Who be asking?" The boy, with a mop of chestnut hair, short pants, and scabby knees, stopped and glared at the strange girl in clothes the likes of which he had only glimpsed on moneyed folk. Penny told him that Mrs. O'Malley wanted a word with him, then turned and charged down the hall towards the kitchen.

A little later Penny came back with a tray, set with two cups and biscuits on a plate. "Here it is." She placed the tray on the small table in front of Mrs. O'Malley and watched as the blind woman poured out the tea with ease and grace. There was no sign of the boy named Jamie.

"Now, my dear, to what do I owe this visit?"

"I want to do my history paper on the books that Ireland rescued. Would you help me?"

"I can think of nothing I'd like more." Mrs. O'Malley leaned in towards the heat of the fire as if warming to the tale to come.

Time passed, but not in the usual way. In the blink of an eye an hour had gone by, and, as if by magic, there in the doorway stood Duncan.

"Are you mad, girl?" Duncan's hair stuck out in all directions from under his cap. His eyes were as round as saucers, and his lips were pulled so tight that they almost disappeared. Jamie had called from the public telephone in the bathhouse at the end of the road. And thank the Lord for small mercies, it was Sally who had answered. Jamie had shouted into the telephone, "Mrs. O'Malley's told me to ring up. There's a wee girl visiting by the name of Pent-a-pee and Mrs. O'Malley says it's best if Duncan comes and collects her." Duncan had his cap on his head before Sally had put the telephone receiver back in the box.

"Forgive me, darlin' girl," said Mrs. O'Malley to Penny. "But I did send for Duncan to fetch you home."

Penny looked out the window. It was pitch black outside. Where had the time gone?

"You did right to call me, Ma. I'll see her home safe. But I can't stop and visit. Mrs. Underhill is due home any time. We'll all be in for it if this gets out."

Penny's lips quivered. She hadn't meant to get anyone into trouble. She pulled on her coat, then gathered up her papers and put them in her school bag.

Mrs. O'Malley reached her hand out to Penny. "Sure as rain, you'll do fine. As for you, my son, you'll not speak harshly to the girl."

Duncan kept his word. He didn't speak harshly to Penny. He didn't speak at all. Not a word all the way home.

Sally, with a shawl wrapped around her, stood in the dark holding open the back door.

"Quick," she whispered. "Mrs. Underhill and Miss Colleen are just in. They're in the sitting room waiting on a cold supper. Cook has it on trays."

Duncan slipped past the two and disappeared up the back stairs. Penny meant to slip past Sally, too.

"Just a wee minute." Sally caught hold of Penny's shoulders, and for a moment Penny thought she was about to get a good shake. Instead, Sally gave Penny a tight hug, then looked right into her green eyes. "What got into your head, girl? Are you mad? Young girls do not go walking about all areas of town at night. You gave us a fright, so ya did."

"I'm sorry. I stayed too long. I didn't mean to cause an upset, really I didn't. In Halifax I always took care of myself, and my sisters, too." Penny fought back tears. It was so, so, so frustrating. Everyone treated her as if she were a child, and a stupid child at that!

"This is not Halifax." Sally had been worried, not only for Penny's safety but for Duncan's position, and her own, too. But something in Penny's sad eyes made her stop. "Oh darlin', just promise me you'll never go off like that again."

"I promise."

"Go up the back way and get changed. I'll tell your grandmother that you are just finishing up your homework and you'll be down soon to say goodnight. Go!"

Penny scooted up the stairs, taking two at a time. As she hung up her school uniform, she reached into a pocket and unfolded the paper Miss Major had given her. In a beautiful, scripted hand Penny read, *Dr. Harold Finn, History Professor, McGill University.*

"Are you sure about this?" Gwen and Penny stood in the grand stone entrance to McGill University. Penny nodded. It had taken her two days to write down everything that Mrs. O'Malley had told her, and now she had to see if it was right.

Both girls had been given permission to visit the university. Grandmother, distracted with the problems of overcrowding at the hospital, had agreed when she'd heard that Miss Major had recommended Dr. Finn. Gwen's mother had agreed when she'd heard that Mrs. Underhill had agreed. Sally thought the whole thing sounded fishy, but she'd written out the directions to McGill all the same.

"Can I help you, girls?" A dour-faced woman wearing a sober blue suit spoke so loudly that Penny and Gwen nearly leapt out of their skins.

"We are looking for Dr. Finn." Gwen used her polite, Miss Potter's School voice.

"History Department. Top floor. Take the stairs to the right." The woman turned and walked away.

They climbed and climbed and climbed until they were beginning to feel hopelessly lost.

"Do . . . you . . . suppose . . . Dr. Finn lives in Heaven?" Gwen, hand over hand, used the wooden handrail to pull herself up the steps.

Penny was too puffed out to answer. This last set of winding stone steps led to a closed oak door. "It looks like a door that would lead to a dungeon," she said.

"Dungeons are down in the cellar, not up in the rafters," huffed Gwen. "Go on, then." Gwen nudged her.

Tentatively, Penny knocked on the professor's door.

"Harder," whispered Gwen.

Penny gave the door four sharp raps.

"Come in."

They looked at each other, took in a deep breath, and opened the door.

They didn't laugh, although it was hard not to. Dr. Finn was a small, round man with wisps of silver hair poking out all over his head, including his ears and nose. He had bushy white eyebrows, a matching moustache, and a cap of tousled white hair. He looked like a character in a picture book.

"Are you girls lost?" the man asked, but not unkindly, as he slipped a pencil into his tangled web of bushy hair. Another pencil peeked out from behind his ear, and one seemed to be sticking up from the top of his head.

Penny found her voice first. "Are you Dr. Finn?"

"I am. And who is asking?"

"My name is Penny Reid, and this is my friend, Gwen Parker-Jones."

"It looks like a door that would lead to a dungeon."

"How do you do? What can I do for you?"

"Miss Major—"

"Maud?"

"Pardon?"

"Maud Major? Is that who you mean?"

Penny and Gwen looked at each other. Gwen slapped her hand over her mouth to keep from giggling. It had never occurred to them that Miss Major even *had* a first name.

"Miss Major teaches at our school," Gwen managed to say.

"Great Scott! Well, why didn't you say so in the first place?" The man was positively beaming. "Maudie's a good friend of mine. Lovely family. Sit, sit. So you are Maudie's students. Good, good. Anything I can do to help. Come, come girls, don't sit there like frogs on a log. Catching flies, are you?"

Penny's mouth gaped open. She shut it.

"I, or I mean Miss Major, said that you were an expert in Irish history." Penny found her voice, small though it was.

"Yes, yes. So they tell me. Of course, I don't believe everything I hear."

"Pardon?" Penny was confused.

"If you like, you are pardoned."

This was all terribly confusing. Penny looked at Gwen, who shrugged. Well, there was nothing for it but to charge ahead.

"I wrote an essay, and I was hoping you would read it."

"Pass it over. Come, come." Dr. Finn drew a pencil out of his hair and licked the nib, as though eagerly anticipating a mistake.

Penny opened her schoolbag and handed Dr. Finn three sheets of paper. Dr. Finn read Penny's essay while he puffed hard on an unlit pipe. "Hummmm," the professor muttered. Then, "Ahhhhhh." Followed by, "Extraordinary! How did you come by this?"

"Is it not true?" Penny's eyes widened with alarm.

"Now the word *true* is a funny thing. Ancient history is but a collection of fragmented events that we historians try to piece together. Indeed, if anything of such a faraway past is true, then why not this? Now tell me, what is your source?"

"Who."

"Who?"

"*Who* is my source, not *what* is my source," said Penny, who was also getting quite muddled.

"Your *what* is a *who*?" The professor nearly leaped out of his chair. "I must meet this *who*. Who is *who*?"

"Do you mean Mrs. O'Malley?" Penny asked, uncertainly.

"Ah, the *who* has a name. Are you telling me that a Mrs. O'Malley gave you this information? Smashing! I would like to make the acquaintance of this mysterious Mrs. O'Malley."

Ten minutes later the two girls stumbled down the steps and out of the building, both in fits of laughter. A blast of fall air sobered them up some.

"Are you going to give it to your grandmother to read?" asked Gwen as she did up the top button of her coat.

Penny dithered then kicked a pebble ahead of her as the two girls walked across the campus. What if Grandmother thought it was all nonsense—a silly make-believe story about the Irish? She didn't think she could bear that right now.

"Grandma is really busy with her hospital work."

At the corner Gwen waved goodbye as Penny trudged up the hill towards home.

CHAPTER N° 8

The next Sunday afternoon was grey and dull. Grandmother and Aunt Colleen sat in the winged chairs by the fire. Grandmother was reading the newspaper while Aunt Colleen was knitting. Penny, curled up on the window seat, was trying to read Milton's *Paradise Lost,* but it was just so hard to concentrate. It would have been easier if she could have read a story out of her *Girl's Own* book, but Grandmother frowned on reading frivolous stories on a Sunday. Penny fogged up a patch of glass with her breath and wrote *Papa* in big letters. Underneath, in smaller letters, she wrote *Emily* and *Maggie,* and then, in teeny-tiny letters, *Penny.*

"There's more in the paper about Quebec breaking away from Confederation. Separation indeed. It's this war and conscription. Mark my word, forcing young men into this war will split this country in two." Grandmother gave a long, sad sigh before putting aside the newspaper. "Penny, I forgot to mention that your sisters have received the package we sent them. Your aunt in Toronto says that both Maggie and Emily are well, although Maggie has yet to say a word. I think it is time we brought in a specialist. I shall ask Dr. Sanders for a recommendation. He must know a good doctor in Toronto."

Penny cleaned the glass with her sleeve. After the explosion, Maggie had stopped making sounds. She didn't even make bubbly baby sounds.

"Excuse me, ma'am, this telegram just arrived."

Aunt Colleen lurched forward and gripped the arms of her chair. No one spoke. Duncan stood to Grandmother's left holding a silver tray.

On it lay the cream-coloured telegram and a letter opener.

"Thank you," said Grandmother. Only a slight tremor of her hand betrayed her fears as she expertly sliced open the envelope.

"Oh no." Grandmother's voice caught in her throat.

"Is it about Robert?" Aunt Colleen was as pale as ice.

Grandmother shook her head. A small sigh of relief escaped from Aunt Colleen's lips. Telegrams were hateful things; in times of war they always brought bad news.

"It's from Mrs. Skinner's housekeeper. Mabel Skinner received a telegram yesterday. It's her son, Scott. He was killed at some place called Belcourt."

"That's her only child, and he's only nineteen. He left for the war less than three months ago!" Aunt Colleen's eyes grew wide in alarm. Penny knew that look. As much as her aunt would mourn the death of any young man, she was really thinking that she might have been the one receiving such news. She might have been the one mourning the loss of Robert, her only brother.

"I'd like to go to her, Aunt Penelope. Mabel's husband is in France, too. He's a commander in the Patricias, I think." Aunt Colleen did her best to compose herself, but all the effort in the world could not stop her shoulders from slumping forward.

"Of course you must go. Arthur will drive you."

"No, I'll walk, if you don't mind."

"Good heavens, Colleen, doesn't Mrs. Skinner live on Green Avenue? It's a good ten blocks or more."

"A long walk will do me good. Perhaps I'll stay the night. Oh Penny, tomorrow night is Parents' Night at your school. I shall try not to miss it." Aunt Colleen stood up and stumbled.

Grandmother leapt to her feet and took Aunt Colleen's elbow. "You really must let Arthur drive you, my dear," she whispered.

Aunt Colleen nodded. "Yes, perhaps that's best. Oh, how many more lives will this war take?"

"Thank you, Miss Major, for leading us in prayer for our valiant soldiers serving overseas, and for that rousing chorus of 'God Save the King' and 'O Canada.'" Miss Potter stood behind a portable lectern and graciously motioned to Miss Major, who stood up from the piano and gave a slight bow. Polite applause followed.

"Ladies, parents, welcome to our Parents' Night." Miss Potter positively beamed out to the crowd. "We have decided to do something new this year. Given the quality of history papers turned in, I have decided to award prizes. We will start with the senior girls." There was oohing from the students, who sat on straight-backed chairs in the first four rows. Parents and relatives sat in the rows behind.

Penny looked over her shoulder. Her grandmother sat alone, towards the back of the room. If only Aunt Colleen were there. She had telephoned earlier in the day to say that Mrs. Skinner was in a bad way and she dared not leave. It didn't really matter. What was the point of Parents' Night if one didn't have any parents?

Two senior girls received their certificates of merit. "Now, the middle girls," said Miss Potter.

Gwen reached over and touched Penny's hand. "It doesn't matter if you win or lose. Yours is the best," she whispered. Startled, Penny turned and stared at her friend. She hadn't thought . . . not for a second . . . oh! Her breath went out of her, completely, utterly. She felt herself sway.

"What's wrong with you? You look ill," Gwen whispered.

"My grandmother thinks I wrote an essay on Queen Elizabeth."

"What did you tell her that for?"

"I didn't tell her, it's just that I didn't *not* tell her."

"What?"

"Honourable mention goes to Miss Ruth Knox for her essay on Sir John A. Macdonald, our first prime minister." There was rousing applause as Ruth stood up and accepted a framed certificate.

Please, please don't let me win. I will never tell another fib in my life. Please, please.

"First place goes to Penelope Underhill Reid for the essay entitled, 'The Irish Saved the World.'"

There was, for the briefest moment, stunned silence. Gwen gave Penny a sharp nudge. "Go."

Whispers raced through the crowd.

"That's the Underhill girl. You remember her mother, Elizabeth Underhill."

"Wasn't she the one who ran off and married the Irish fellow?"

"That's the one."

"Well, the apple doesn't fall far from the tree."

"Penny, where are you, dear?" Miss Potter looked out over the crowd. Penny felt Gwen's hand on her back. She was standing. Audrey Hicks, sitting one row ahead, turned and mouthed, "Go on, *Irish*."

"There you are. Come forward, Penelope. As a special treat I am going to ask Penelope to read a paragraph from her essay."

Penny felt faint. No, she felt sick.

She stumbled up to the lectern and whispered to Miss Potter, "I can't . . ."

"Not to worry, dear," Miss Potter whispered into Penny's ear. "I brought your essay. Just read the second paragraph. I have circled it. There you go." Miss Potter passed her the paper.

Penny's legs wobbled so much her skirt fluttered. She looked down at her essay. The words seemed to race across the page in all directions. Her throat went bone dry. She didn't dare look up in Grandmother's direction, but she could see her out of the corner of her eye. Grandmother

*She didn't dare look up in
Grandmother's direction,
but she could see her out
of the corner of her eye.*

sat as tall and rigid as a pillar of salt. There was no expression on her face, none.

"Take a deep breath, dear," whispered Miss Potter.

"'The Roman Empire fell in 410 A.D. With the sacking of Rome, most of the great books of history were at risk of disappearing altogether. We will never know what was lost. Some books were saved. They were taken to a faraway country where monks and scribes copied the books and kept them safe until the world was ready to take them back. The books included Virgil's *Aeneid,* the works of Plato, the Greek *Iliad,* and . . . the Bible. The country these books were taken to was . . . Ireland.'" Penny stopped. The room was deathly silent.

"Thank you, Penny. I have a note that I would like to read out loud. It is from Professor Finn of McGill University, to our own Miss Major," said Miss Potter.

"'Dear Miss Major,' he writes. 'I would like to congratulate you on having Miss Reid as a student. I read her work with great pleasure. Sincerely, Dr. Harold Finn, History Professor, McGill University.'"

The applause started in the back.

"Ladies, parents, and guests, we will have a break now. Please join us for refreshments." Gracious as ever, Miss Potter motioned to the study, where the senior girls were getting ready to serve tea, coffee, and punch.

Penny, clutching her essay and hardly daring to look up, walked slowly towards Grandmother. Her feet felt like lead weights. Several parents stopped to congratulate her grandmother. She overheard one lady say, "Mrs. Underhill, what a charming granddaughter you have." *Charming*? Someone thought she was charming! No matter. Grandmother smiled, but it was a polite smile, not a real smile.

When Penny was a mere arm's length away, a large woman pushed right in front of her.

"Mrs. Underhill, how nice to see you. Perhaps you remember me. I'm Martha Hicks, and this is my daughter Audrey."

Audrey stood beside her mother, shifting her weight from foot to foot. Mrs. Hicks gave Audrey a sharp poke with her elbow and Audrey came to a swift halt, mid-shift.

"I knew your daughter Elizabeth. We were in class together. I must say that we were all horrified when dear Elizabeth ran off with that dreadful Irishman. Now here you are, raising her child. Really, you are a wonder." Mrs. Hicks gushed and flapped her hands about.

Penny took in a sharp breath and looked from Grandmother to Mrs. Hicks. She felt the blood rush to her head. If she could have melted right into the floor, she would have. Audrey gave Penny a big, cheesy smile.

"*I* am a wonder?" Grandmother looked from mother to daughter then back to mother again. Her eyes took in everything.

"Oh, indeed." Mrs. Hicks leaned in and added, "Caring for a child at your age, and one with such little regard for propriety. Irish indeed! I just want you to know how much I admire you. And I hear there are two other children as well. My, my."

Like a battleship tuning its big gun and taking aim, Grandmother slowly lifted her chin, stared into the woman's dull eyes, and spoke in a low, slow, direct voice. "The wonder is not in me but in my granddaughter. I have been given many blessings in my life, and I consider *all* my granddaughters to be the greatest of those blessings. As for Penelope being half Irish, may I remind you that she is also half English and *all* Canadian, and I am grateful for every single part—the Irish part included!"

"I didn't mean . . . of course . . . I meant to say . . ." Mrs. Hicks's eyes grew big and round and bits of spittle sprayed from her mouth.

"I know exactly what you meant to say." At no point did Grandmother raise her voice above a whisper, and yet every word had the impact of a cannonball hurtling through the air.

Mrs. Hicks reeled backwards. The heel of her shoe landed on one of Audrey's big feet. The girl let out a shriek that would have sent a pig into flight. The room turned to gape at Mrs. Hicks while her daughter hopped around on one foot. Miss Potter gasped. Like a torpedoed ship, Mrs. Hicks seemed to sink down, down, and down some more.

Grandmother turned and settled her sparkly blue eyes on Penny. "Now, Penny dear, perhaps you could show me around your school."

Penny swallowed hard and nodded. Grandmother and granddaughter walked side by side down the hall.

"This is the music room," said Penny. "And this is where I have my history class." She pointed to a room across the hall.

"Ah yes, history class." Grandmother smiled. "May I see your history paper?"

Penny looked down. She had forgotten that the paper was still in her hand. Penny handed Grandmother the essay. Across the top, written in Miss Potter's perfectly scripted hand, were the words, "A creative and well-written piece. Great initiative."

"I wrote it for Papa. It was to be his Christmas present," Penny said quietly.

"I might have suggested that you put it into one of Colleen's letters to your father. Your aunt seems inordinately fond of the man," Grandmother added rather wistfully. What did she mean? Of course Aunt Colleen liked Papa. Everybody liked Papa. "But instead, I think perhaps you should give it to him yourself." She handed back the paper.

The wind went right out of Penny. Could it be? "What do you mean, Grandma?"

"I've asked your father—and your sisters too, of course—to come for Christmas."

"Christmas?" It took a minute for the news to sink in. "Oh Grandma, thank you. Thank you." Penny threw her arms around her grandmother.

"Now, now, think about *propriety,* my dear girl." Grandmother's eyes twinkled.

"But why? I mean, why did you change your mind?"

"Let's just say that your Aunt Colleen is very

persuasive. Besides, it seems to me it's about time that I met my two other granddaughters."

"Oh Grandma." Penny hugged her all over again.

Grandmother looked over Penny's shoulder. Mrs. Hicks and Audrey were making a hasty retreat through the front door.

"Come now. Straighten up." Grandmother motioned in Mrs. Hicks's direction. "You will find that people who belittle others come in all different ages and from all different walks of life. In my opinion, it's best if you learn to stand up for yourself as soon as possible. Now, where is your Latin class? Did I mention that your mother was not terribly good at Latin . . . or Greek, come to think of it."

"Really? I'm not very good at Latin or Greek either!"

"Well, I'm glad you mentioned it sooner rather than later," said Grandmother. "I shall put in a call to your tutor, Mr. Davis, first thing in the morning."

Oh darn! And then she remembered Mrs. O'Malley's words: *May the blessings of each day be the blessings you need most.* Grandmother had said that Penny was a blessing to her. Thing was, Grandmother had come into her life when she'd needed her most. "It works both ways," whispered Penny.

"What did you say, dear?" Grandmother turned towards Penny.

"Oh, just that this is the way to the geography room." Penny smiled.

ENDNOTE

Miss Potter's School for Girls is based on Miss Edgar's and Miss Cramp's (ECS), a private girls' school in Montreal, Quebec. It opened in September 1909 at 507 Guy Street (later changed to 2035) and moved to Cedar Avenue in 1949, where it now resides.

The idea that the Irish did in fact save the great books after the fall of the Roman Empire is explored in a wonderful book called How the Irish Saved Civilization *by Thomas Cahill, published by Doubleday. This is an adult book, and while it might be too difficult to read now, it will wait for you.*

The Great War, now called World War I, began in 1914 and ended on November 11, 1918. Sixty thousand Canadian lives were lost. On the heels of the war came a flu brought home by returning soldiers in the spring and summer of 1918. It killed a further thirty to fifty thousand Canadians and anywhere from fifteen to twenty million people worldwide.

Acknowledgements

Barbara Berson, editor of the Our Canadian Girl series

Anne Dublin

Rennie MacLeod, librarian of Miss Edgar's
and Miss Cramp's School, Montreal

Melanie Adelson and Chloé Isabella Kangas-Miller,
students of ECS

Marc Chiasson, City of Verdun

Deven Ghodiwala, computer whiz

Robert Hickey, editorial assistant

Catherine Marjoribanks, copy editor

Dear Reader,

Welcome back to the continuing adventures
of Our Canadian Girl! It's been another
exciting year for the series, with ten girls'
stories published and two more on the way!
In January you'll meet Keeley, who moves to
the newly established town of Frank, Alberta,
in 1901, and Millie, a Toronto girl spending
the summer of 1914 in the Kawarthas.

So please keep on reading. And do stay in
touch. Write to us, log on to our website.
We love to hear from you!

Sincerely,
Barbara Berson
Editor

Canada's

1608
Samuel de Champlain establishes the first fortified trading post at Quebec.

1759
The British defeat the French in the Battle of the Plains of Abraham.

1812
The United States declares war against Canada.

1845
The expedition of Sir John Franklin to the Arctic ends when the ship is frozen in the pack ice; the fate of its crew remains a mystery.

1869
Louis Riel leads his Métis followers in the Red River Rebellion.

1871
British Columbia joins Canada.

1755
The British expel the entire French population of Acadia (today's Maritime provinces), sending them into exile.

1776
The 13 Colonies revolt against Britain, and the Loyalists flee to Canada.

1837
Calling for responsible government, the Patriotes, following Louis-Joseph Papineau, rebel in Lower Canada; William Lyon Mackenzie leads the uprising in Upper Canada.

1867
New Brunswick, Nova Scotia and the United Province of Canada come together in Confederation to form the Dominion of Canada.

1870
Manitoba joins Canada. The Northwest Territories become an official territory of Canada.

1784
Rachel

Timeline

1885
At Craigellachie, British Columbia, the last spike is driven to complete the building of the Canadian Pacific Railway.

1898
The Yukon Territory becomes an official territory of Canada.

1914
Britain declares war on Germany, and Canada, because of its ties to Britain, is at war too.

1918
As a result of the Wartime Elections Act, the women of Canada are given the right to vote in federal elections.

1945
World War II ends conclusively with the dropping of atomic bombs on Hiroshima and Nagasaki.

1873
Prince Edward Island joins Canada.

1896
Gold is discovered on Bonanza Creek, a tributary of the Klondike River.

1905
Alberta and Saskatchewan join Canada.

1917
In the Halifax harbour, two ships collide, causing an explosion that leaves more than 1,600 dead and 9,000 injured.

1939
Canada declares war on Germany seven days after war is declared by Britain and France.

1949
Newfoundland, under the leadership of Joey Smallwood, joins Canada.

1897
Emily

1885
Marie-Claire

1918
Penelope

Don't miss your chance to meet all the girls in the Our Canadian Girl series...

EMILY: BUILDING BRIDGES

In *Emily: Building Bridges*, Hing's family finally arrives and Emily at last meets Mei Yuk, Hing's daughter. After a rocky start, the two girls become fast friends. But as Emily begins to include Mei Yuk in her social life, she finds things changing between her and Alice, her best friend. Inspired by her art teacher, a young Emily Carr, Emily learns the importance of staying true to oneself.

ISBN 0-14-301461-7

MARIE-CLAIRE: VISITORS

Marie-Claire is facing the consequences, both good and bad, of her generous offer to house the Linteaus, a family who lost their home in a fire. While their presence fills the house with the vitality and laughter missing since the death of Emilie, it's a small house and there are just too many people living in it. Marie-Claire decides to take matters into her own hands.

ISBN 0-14-301485-4

RACHEL: CERTIFICATE OF FREEDOM

Racial tension is at a boiling point in Shelbourne, Nova Scotia, as white delisted soldiers become desperate for work. In this third installment of Rachel's story, the unthinkable happens—on the pretense of checking their certificates of freedom, one such former soldier spirits Rachel and her mother away from their home and sells them back into servitude. Determined to reclaim her freedom and her home, Rachel plots her escape, with the help of an unlikely ally.

ISBN 0-14-301462-5

www.ourcanadiangirl.ca

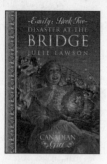

EMILY: DISASTER AT THE BRIDGE

Emily Murdoch is looking forward to the four-day celebration of Queen Victoria's birthday. On May 26, Emily, her family and friends climb on board streetcars for the ride to Esquimalt to witness the climax of the holiday celebrations. As Car 16 rolls onto the Point Ellice Bridge, the centre span of the bridge collapses, and the streetcar—packed with more than 120 passengers—plunges into the Gorge.

ISBN 0-14-331206-5

MARIE-CLAIRE: A SEASON OF SORROW

Of the 3,200 people who died during the smallpox epidemic in 1885, 2,500 of them were children under the age of 10. In *A Season of Sorrow*, smallpox descends upon Marie-Claire and her family. How they, their community and the church cope with the epidemic, as well as with the controversial vaccine meant to guard against it, is the focus of this story.

ISBN 0-14-331209-X

PENELOPE: THE GLASS CASTLE

In the wake of the Halifax Explosion of 1917, Penny's father must make a tough decision. Faced with the difficulty of finding housing for his three daughters, Papa sends Emily and Maggie to his sister's home in Montreal. Penny, however, must live with Grandmama in Montreal. This decision devastates Penny as the life she is offered is not what she imagined.

ISBN 0-14-331207-3

RACHEL: THE MAYBE HOUSE

Rachel's wish for a house to call her own is granted, thanks to her stepfather Titan's hard work. And her determination to learn to read and write also begins to bear fruit. But the atmosphere in Shelbourne, Nova Scotia, is increasingly intolerant as delisted white soldiers, unable to find work, begin to look with resentment upon their black neighbours.

ISBN 0-14-331208-1

OUR CANADIAN *Girl*

ANGELIQUE:
BUFFALO HUNT
ISBN 0-14-100271-9

EMILY: ACROSS THE
JAMES BAY BRIDGE
ISBN 0-14-100250-6

ELIZABETH: BLESS
THIS HOUSE
ISBN 0-14-100251-4

ELLEN: HOBO JUNGLE
ISBN 0-14-100270-0

IZZIE: THE CHRISTMAS
THAT ALMOST WASN'T
ISBN 0-14-100272-7

LISA: OVERLAND
TO CARIBOO
ISBN 0-14-100327-8

MARGIT: HOME FREE
ISBN 0-14-331200-6

MARIE-CLAIRE: DARK SPRING
ISBN 0-14-100328-6

PENELOPE: TERROR IN
THE HARBOUR
ISBN 0-14-100329-4

RACHEL: A MIGHTY
BIG IMAGINING
ISBN 0-14-100252-2

www.ourcanadiangirl.ca

Check out the
Our Canadian Girl website

Fun Stuff

- E-cards
- Prizes
- Activities
- Poll

Fan Area

- Guest Book
- Photo Gallery
- Downloadable *Our Canadian Girl* Tea Party Kit

Features on the girls and more!

www.ourcanadiangirl.ca